Stompy and Mo – Treetop

Written by:

George Kamperis.

Illustrated by:

Michele Kamperis.

For Sam, Sophie and Ollie.

We wish for peace, we wish for joy,
for every little girl and boy.
Work hard and always do your best.
Make time to play, make time to rest.
Be good in everything you say and do,
and good will then return to you.

Copyright:

George and Michele Kamperis - 2017

This book belongs to:...

Mo thought;
I wonder what will I do today.
Where shall I go and what will I play?
Something I like to do from time-to-time,
is to find a tall tree and climb and climb.
When you sit up high and look around,
there's more to see than from the ground.

As Stompy and Mo played happy and free,
Mo stopped beneath the chestnut tree.
Stompy looked back and thought, where is that cat?
She's disappeared just like that.
He looked to the left and then to the right,
but Mo was completely out of sight.

As Stompy walked around the tree,
he wondered, where could Mo be.
Then he heard a whimpering cry,
and there was Mo, way up high.
Stompy said "what are you doing right up there?"
Mo looked down with a worried stare.

"Hey Stompy, look at me,
I've climbed up high into the tree!
The problem is, it's my bad luck,
I can't get down and now I'm stuck!"

Never mind Mo thought; while I think of what to do,
I'll just sit here and enjoy the view.
As Stompy looked up from down below,
the branch Mo clung to began to bow.
Oh dear Mo thought, this was a big mistake,
just as the branch began to break!

In the nick of time as the branch broke free,
Mo leapt higher into the tree.
Oh dear, she thought, I will have to be clever,
or I might be stuck up here forever.

Stompy had really started to worry,
as Alfie and Jane arrived in a hurry.
And in a rapid response to come to Mo's aid,
Alfie called the fire brigade.
The firemen arrived at speed and made a decision,
that they had to attempt a rescue mission!

Firemen have ladders, ropes and equipment like that,
they can easily rescue a stranded cat.
The firemen said "leave it to us,
there's really no need to worry or fuss."
"Stand back" said the Fire Chief. "There's nothing to see.
It's just a cat that's stuck in a tree."

But just as the ladders began to rise,
Stompy had a big surprise!
For as he turned and looked around,
there was Mo back on the ground.

Stompy said "this is really confusing,
and it's really not amusing.
You had us worried half to death,
as we watched from below and held our breath.
Now promise me you won't repeat,
this death defying reckless feat."

Mo's Diary:

<u>May 5th</u>

It's lucky that cats are supposed to have nine lives. I think that I might have used up one of mine today.

For a cat climbing up is so easy compared to coming down. It feels so nice sinking my claws into the soft bark of a tall tree and then higher and higher I go! Then comes the problem – how do I get down?

But somehow I always manage to get back down. I haven't had to be rescued yet, but perhaps I've just been very lucky.

One of my favourite places to explore is Poddington woods. There's lots of lovely tall trees to climb and in the spring time I can hide amongst the bluebells.

I love looking down from rooftops and often spend hours just sitting on the roof of the garden shed.

I once got stuck on the roof of our house. I can't remember how I managed to get up there, but it was hours before Jane and Alfie saw me and helped me in through the loft window.

I suppose that was a kind of rescue!

A funny little poem!

There once was a dog called custard,
who was always terribly flustered.

Even when cooking, he was neither thinking nor looking,
and he fell in a bowl full of custard!

Ordering Information:
www.stompyandmo.com

Printed in the United Kingdom.

ISBN 978-0-9957936-3-7

First Edition